Tales from the Day

Soraya Bodorff

eBook ISBN: 978-1-966003-59-5
Paperback ISBN: 978-1-966003-60-1
Hardback ISBN: 978-1-966003-61-8

A Decade in the San Francisco Mix- 2000-2010

Dedication

To my father, mother and grandmother

In loving memory.

CONTENTS

San Francisco Tales

As a youngish woman of age, I made the decision to try my hand out at the city by the bay "San Francisco." The treat that's got the beat, a lyric I will never forget, Rice a Roni, the San Francisco treat, perhaps I thought I might find gold too? A city that invented a treat, to an alternative, to potatoes with cable cars, allowing people the ability to hang on the sides as you were taken up and down perilous hills that simultaneously included breathtaking views of the bay. It was dreamy, especially for an adult who liked any excuse to relive childhood theme parks. I was sold on the place.

If it didn't work out, I could always jump off the Golden Gate Bridge. A quick, clean, and easily accessible way to end things in 4 seconds flat. I figured I had nothing much to lose. Life was fleeting to me as far as I was concerned.

Previous to this venture, I had descended upon a few other cities around the globe, such as Chicago, New York and Barcelona. I was able to navigate them with limited supplies then; why not now?

Cut to song by Supertramp-Dreamer, You silly little dreamer / So now you put your head in your hands, Oh no… Well you know, well you had it coming to you….

I decided to head out west with a couple of suitcases and the five hundred dollars I had earned from cleaning out the remains of an apartment. Being the daughter of a slumlord, I had some advantages to opportunities, such as a janitor or a painter for tenants, living in disarray, or death. At the tender age of 5, I embarked on my assistant duties. My older sister and I assisted our dad in picking up crushed beer cans, trash, old clothes, and kitchenware left behind by people on the run. After a hard day of work, we would get rewarded with a Mexican coke that costed 25 cents. My dad's favorite saying throughout my childhood and adulthood is, "It’s better than a swift kick in the ass.” I got used to the saying and figured he was right that I’d rather the grunt work than the sting of being kicked in the rear.

Arriving at the Bay

Having a natural affinity for adventure and a sweet spot for cities rich in history, magical backdrops, and cable cars, I jumped into the assignment. First stop: a friend's couch and the Craigslist job link/classifieds rooms for rent page.

I made my way to an old college roommate's place; I had

limited time to find a place, so I knew the pressure was on. I scoured the listings, hoping something that seemed doable would present itself. I went on rounds of interviews of a wide variety. First, I considered the Castro, it was centrally located, colorful, and upbeat. Growing up in Montrose, Houston, I was no stranger to the gay men's underground club scene. During my helper days as a cleaner, I witnessed many characters in the apartments who frequented a nightclub across the street called Chutes & Ladders. It was covered in aluminum siding with no windows from the outside. I suppose the naming made sense, it was like a chute with no ladder if you ask me. Either way, I had been around the types and was open to the Castro option. I met with Dottie, a middle-aged graphic designer who had carpal tunnel and wore a sling on her hand because of it. She had a room to rent and, during our interview, said she was more than okay with me bringing in men at my leisure. In other words, she didn't mind if I was a trollop. I decided to pass on Dottie. I caught a weird vibe and pressed on to other options with more people. Somehow, I thought I might be better off in groups rather than one sling-carrying stranger with a seemed passion for promiscuity.

Adalgisa Nights

I enrolled in a graphic design program, figuring I had a creative eye and a flair for composition and color. Getting out of Cowtown, Houston, was my agenda, and it worked. The country's Western fashion was enough ammo to fuel nausea for weeks, and don't get me started on the music- If I had to choose, I would pick Miguel Miggs over ZZ tops, but that's just me. The search for a room was carrying on longer than expected, so I had to couch surf at my distant cousin's place. I was a repeat offender, breaking the overstayed visitor card two times in a row. Third times a charm didn't seem like a fun catchphrase at this point, and as luck played out, I found a room in the distant sunset part of town. It was just a 10-minute bus ride to Ocean Beach. I rented a room from a Brazilian lady, Adalgisa. She had flaming red corkscrew curly hair, with a face reminiscent of the late Groucho Marks, minus the mustache. She rented me her bedroom while she inhabited the living room area. Pretty typical setup in places like San Francisco or New York. I was on a collegiate budget and well, this was as good as I could find. Adalgisa liked to hit the brown drink. During our interview, I noticed she was tossing a few back, but I didn't read into it. I had started my graphics training, and most nights, I would come back to the flat and find her dancing pirouettes in a loose-fitting negligee with her tiny poodle in tow while listening to samba beats. I am a real fan of Brian Eno, especially his samba days, so I enjoyed her upbeat attitude and zest for dancing unabashedly. I wanted to mesh with her, so I stomached the stiff whisky drink out of camaraderie.

As time moved on, she ended up renting her walk-in closet to another Brazilian named Juan. He wasn't a petite man by any means, but he was able to cram a cot, a phone jack, and a mini-25 TV into the crevice. At first, it was a bit jarring, not expecting to see any life inside such a cramped space. Usually, closets are just for jackets, but we were in San Francisco after all; the rent was high, and people had to get by on what they could. The Brazilian beats ended as the landlord snuffed us all out, I had to vacate immediately. It was a bum deal, but I had to press on. I packed up my computer and a few bags and threw them into the back of my cousin's husband's truck, back to couch surfing. This was the fourth time and well, I was getting the hang of it. I kept hearing the lyrics from the second time around though this was the fourth, I suppose that song is just so damn catchy, and I was hoping it might be like they say, "It's not like the first time, talk about the second time, let's do it one more time… Oh Shalimar you got it right, You can make it on your own!!!" I just love the bay so much I would do anything to keep trying. It was truly my place. I felt alive, magical, and inspired every day by my bus rides full of mixed media people, fights amongst people with strollers, and pushy Asians who knew how to steal seats and push hard. I learned how to push and pull amongst the California bus line that went up and down hills like a slip and slide, It was cheap entertainment at its best. I loved it.

Tempin It

After training with the Academy for three years, I decided to launch into the work scene, so I hit the want ads. I floated in between office support, managing calendars for biotechnology cos', marketing conglomerates, non-profit foundations, advertising agencies, law firms, and the most unusual - a San Francisco gem, an adult video production house. I was hired as a production manager for the graphics /video dept. Many aspects of the gig were unusual, bizarre, and outlandish. The production house was a loft space located smack dab in the "Tenderloin" of 6th and Market Street. It is San Francisco's roughest area; you avoided it by day and night unless you were looking to score a drug deal. The operation housed a customer service center team that worked in the cellar of the building. Most of the employees looked like creatures from a Frankenstein movie, some humpbacks, midgets, and the

LGBT community. I didn't shy away from it. I liked the circus-like feel, one of my favorite books being "Geek Love" by Katherine Dunn. It must be the adventurer in me. I saw it as a chance to experience the book in person.

My everyday walk consisted of jumping across crack heads collection of paraphernalia that was openly sprawled out for use, not an effect. I could see the users appeared disheveled, their mouths looked dark purple, and their eyes, which I tried to avoid, were dark too, but mostly their behavior was very animalistic. They were positioned on the ground most days, scattering around their loot in the frog yoga pose. I would head into my desk area while I passed dildos propped up on the sides of cubicles as I assumed were for decor or a welcome mat, so to speak. When I needed to get my printouts from the printer, I would bump into old videos they must have discarded or perhaps in the middle of considering. It wasn't easy to keep a straight face as "Debbie did Dallas" or "Little Orphan Tranny" were in your face. I had to compose myself. I needed a paycheck, so I stomached the laughter inside.

The outfit would run meetings with the team, which consisted of a mix of marketers, coders, brand experts, and other players who contributed to ideas and movements that kept the underground videos afloat. I did my best to try to act natural whilst the title-naming discussions went on but it wasn't easy. "Trannie Got Your Gun," "Little Oral Annie," "Honey, I Blew Everyone" to name a few. I had to get used to this act, I kept telling myself, you need to pretend this is just like changing underwear or crossing the street - normal, ordinary... I was getting paid a lot to be there, I needed to pull this off, my 1500 a month Nob Hill one room apt didn't pay for itself. I would distract my impulse to laugh by looking out the conference room window at other people as a tactic of diversion to repel the laughter.

My job was to oversee the graphics dept, so I did my best to go over and linger above the editors with demands while they sliced and diced, again seeing people go at it in compromising positions all day long and having to discuss it in detail really did take its toll. I couldn't help to soak in the vibe and wanting to be one of the main characters, it just felt right. Why can’t I be moaning right now instead of watching these other people have the time of their lives? Didn't seem fair, but I kept the charade going for a while until I got fired. I wasn't the right fit for the underground scene I suppose. My manager apparently was into S&M and wore one of those rings people wear to identify themselves as master or slave. I did get to create a creative campaign for Christmas at least, so I felt some gratification by contributing. I came upon a “Midnight Queer” title among a few others.

Cyber dating; My try with a Gap Model with a 90's vibe

I was feeling restless, and my jaunts hanging around casually at various venues around town wasn't resulting in any par amour relations. I was lonely and craved a companion other than the plastic memorabilia from the production house. I longed for a human touch, specifically from a man; man's hands are like no other to me. I just wasn't attracted to slender feminine hands, I had those already, who needed another pair? It was the year 2000, and I decided to buck up and try the latest craze of internet dating. I went through scores of listings. I decided to role-play as a casting director. I was looking to fulfill my fantasy of being Lois Lane from the movie Superman. I needed a blue-eyed guy with muscles who looked good in a onesie and had a knack for being a hero.

I selected this guy named Clyde, and he claimed he had done some modeling for the Gap.His headshot was uber cheesy reminiscent of a glamour shot from the 90's. We met at the Fairmont Hotel, which was the setting for the series Hotel in the 1980's. It all felt dated: the guy, the setting, his crew cut glazed over by, I suspect, cheap gel, and most of all, the fresh smell of axe body spray. We had a few drinks and bonded over the coincidence that we both grew up in the same religious cult, sharing stories of peddling literature door to door as a youth. He suggested we go to the Castro, and I said okay. Should have suspected it at this point, but his sparkling blue eyes had drawn me in for the moment. As we entered the first bar called "The Edge," I noticed it was the atypical gay bar scene, same leather daddy and tranny's. As we made our way to the smoke-induced dance floor, a song from Erasure started to play; it was Oh L 'Amour. Clyde threw off his plethora jacket and started to swing around wildly, singing the lyrics with gusto. He was thrusting his hips back and forth, left and right. However dark it was, I noticed a bulge in his pants, beginning to submerge. The size was reminiscent of a security guard or police officer's swagger stick.

Suddenly, he started to get approached by one gay man after the next. I started to look around the room, however hard it was to see due to the flashing strobe lights, and noticed all eyes were on Superman. He turned down the admirers, but I saw the twinkle in his bisexual eye. He was enjoying it.

I decided to cut my losses and I jumped into a cab and high tailed it home. I never said or heard from Clyde again. Back to square one…

Crazy Elaina

I decided to try my hand at joining a luxury fitness club called the Bay Club. It required a steep joining fee but I thought it might be worth the chance. I was dedicated to fitness either way, so it was an idea. I would attend nightly classes after my temp day jobs and sometimes mixers that gave me opportunities to meet members. I ended up meeting Elaina, an overly friendly 25-year-old who worked in the cafe. She instantaneously befriended me after simple chit-chat and gave me her number pretty quickly. I was looking for girlfriends to get out with, and figured she was healthy working at a gym. Later, I found out otherwise. She was a runner and a sex junkie with a voracious appetite for outrageous behavior. She invited me out to the Marina district for a night on the prowl. I had no idea what crazy was until I met the likes of her. She would approach men on the streets, while we were crossing streets and even passersby cars. Her tag line was "I'd do a doorknob and apparently, she did. Crazy Elaina would walk away with 5 or 6 numbers a night and would make out with at last 4 or 5 random men on every given night we went out. The first time I saw her do it I was shocked, but started to get used to it, then I started to feel nauseated by the sight of her antics. It was traumatic to see her sticking her tongue down so many strangers' throats.

One night we tried the North Beach area and she jumped into a limousine that was passing by, filled with drunken people. She tried to get me into the mix but I wasn't into that type of ride.

I decided to cut my losses with her too. It was more than repulsion, it was outrageously tragic. I remained a member of the club for the following five years. She must have dropped off somewhere in between that time never saw her again. Her memory will not be etched out in my recollections as I remember her slamming her tongue down the throats of countless victims. I am a fan of horror films but usually the protagonist gets some sort of penance or limb cutoff, but she was like an octopus vampire. I try to take the good part of the relationship, we had formed a regular run club on the fitness floor. I became a runner, a good skill.

Back to square one, scratch that one from the pool.

Loving the wrong Jew

As time drew on, I met a lady with a French last name who wanted to show me around. Marchant was from around the area, so I figured I'd get tips from a local, which was usually best. She introduced me to a cigar bar located in the heart of North Beach that featured live music acts with Latin themes. Merchant and I embarked on a seemingly normal friendship in layman's terms. Every Saturday night we began to meet at the club, partner-danced with a variety of Latin men, mostly Cuban or Mexican. Nothing out of the ordinary happened until an unexpected chance encounter. It was a typical Saturday foggy night. I arrived early and sat down at a table in a room adjacent to the bar intended for the performers area when the time was right. Suddenly a tall, lanky long-nosed man wearing a Cuban cabana shirt that was unbuttoned halfway down his chest sat across the table from me. He introduced himself as Gershon, the drummer for the music act. He proceeded to ask me the stereotypical pick up lines like "Come here often", "Are you alone tonight", "Where are you from", "What brings you here" (pretty nosy stranger, no pun intended in relation to his Jewish honker). I've come across many a strangers during my time at lounges that ask a series of questions, as if you are on trial or a suspect for a crime. I usually answer honestly unless I'm in the mood for theatrical play. During my college days, some of my thespian friends and I used to enjoy creating false identities including accents when we met random people just to make it more interesting and perhaps practice our acting skills. I liked playing the Spanish fly from Spain, I would use Charo as my name and pretend all I liked to do is dance the cha-cha. I would present myself as a professional dancer that was in town for a performance, and even take it as far as showing them a sample of my act by performing dance routines on spot.

The musician, Gershon (son of Moses in Hebrew) proceeded to offer me a drink with his complimentary drink tickets. I accepted but deep down, I could already see he was tacky and low-end. I couldn't help be reminded of "A Night at the

Roxbury." He was the Jewish version with no wing man, and no dance moves. As the night grew on, I somehow ended up with Gershon, it must have been my impaired judgement due to the alcohol, must have been seeing triple. Either way I found myself at a North Beach apartment. It was a dingy apartment, collegiate status at best. I scanned the room and noticed his bad taste immediately, it didn't take much to see he lived on pins and needles. I decided to accept it, and live in the bohemian rhapsody as he offered me a "beer". There was some small talk related to who he was, apparently he had studied at Berkeley received some music diploma and taught kids how to play drums while playing in three other bands, he also played the congas. One thing led to another and we ended up in bed. He wasn't able to perform and I should have seen that as relief but I was intoxicated, out of my head. The following day he cooked me breakfast which seemed to be an indication that he was looking to be somewhat friendly, however that's probably as far as he could go on his below average pocketbook. Upon reflection I interpret my willingness to participate with such a type as living out a juvenile fantasy of wanting to be a drummer myself. I had always dreamed of picking the instrument up as a teen, never pursued it so I was living vicariously, or that's how I rationalize the bad decisions anyway.

We parted ways and I headed back to my own place accepting it as just another one of those nights. Gershon ended following up a few days later looking to meet again. At that time, I lived in the heart of Nob Hill just blocks away from the Fairmont Hotel and across the street from the famous Grace Cathedral. One Saturday night he contacted me saying he just ended playing a gig from the Fairmont. Apparently his bands played random events around town, weddings, bar mitzvahs, birthday parties, etc. He reminded me of Adam Sandler from the wedding singer, even resembled him with his Jewish looks. I invited him into my place and things ended up getting horizontal. It was the first time I had ever been with a 6 ft Jewish man. I am somewhat petite in stature so sleeping with him was challenging. He wasn't heavy but tall and large. He would play the bongos on my backside after intercourse so that was definitely something different. His hands knew how to move but it really wasn't that satisfying for me other than I remember laughing at those, time must have been delirious from his overwhelming bravado. I had a pet name for his genitalia, I called him bagel balls in secret or in private with friends. Eventually bagel balls revealed that he had been recently released from the Bette Ford clinic for his addiction to cocaine. I wasn't a user and never had been so I accepted his situation but should have been the reason to run for the hills with that information. A naive 30 yr old woman with some dating experience. I had one other serious boyfriend in the past, an English cyclist. I knew what to expect from casual meetings. The relation was somewhat sweet at first, he had his nicknames for me too like my little Swedish fish, El pirate and my least favorite was turdling. He wasn't exactly a sophisticated man to say the least. Again, must have been out of my head or looking for a story.

I lived steps away from the North Beach district and often times music festivals would occur. We headed to one the following day and that's when it started to dawn on me that this guy was a player, and not in a good way. Many different women started to approach him and when this happened, he would lose grip of my hand and introduce me as his friend. It was pretty awkward and tacky. I was young and impressionable and since I had slept with him must have felt a tie.

As our sex life continued, he started to want to do things I wasn't interested in. I was open to different positions and some light role play but when he started to suggest back door stuff, I just wasn't into it. I wasn't a fan of the back door. When it had happened to me before, it was usually when a guy claimed it was an accident or a mistake. I knew differently, they were gay men that just didn't want to admit it. I understand the physics behind why they say they like to do it as far as feeling and euphoria go, but if that's the case why not just date a gay man who likes the same thing? I never understood their point of view. It would be easier for them to get what they want, they would be on the same page. Why do straight women who enjoy regular intercourse have to be subjected to their preference? I suggested he just come out and hit the Castro, it was minutes away and always open.

The affair lasted for over three years. It mostly ended on a downward spiral and the the finale, with him hitting on my 65-year-old next-door neighbor one night. He had come over one night and my neighbor and close friend, who was a financial analyst for a large company, had just called letting me know her cat died. He encouraged me to call and invite her over for support. I thought it was innocent. They were both pot heads so they smoked out while I was busy doing something around the apartment. I noticed he was being friendly towards her, even touched her leg at one point but disregarded it. The following day, Tobi let me know he had somehow managed to get her number and texted her. I think he looked into my contacts in my phone at one point and decided to take a chance. When I confronted him, I let him know she wasn't interested and laughed in his face. She was well off and drove a Porsche. Guys like that were looking to panty-up regardless of age. That was the end of the affair with Bagel balls.

The Iranian Set Up

Having to accept another round of defeat, I plugged away and hoped something new would come my way. I wasn't giving up that easy, " Be a strong little viking" would re-emerge from my subconscious as it had been drilled into me from my Swedish slumlord dad. If Leif Erikson could settle greenland, why couldn't I at least settle my libido? I needed to live up to my viking heritage and forge forward to the great unknown or as it would be the next san francisco district, chinatown.

Nestled in between grant/stockton street I found a new apartment to rent. It was a Victorian, facing California street and across from the Ritz Carlton hotel. Being a creature of habit I must have felt at home being across from historical monuments. The charming view of the bay was captivating, every morning I had a view of the bay, mesmerizing ships, boats and airplanes flying around. I had my window propped open in the kitchen, and I could hear the Chinese guzeng playing in the backdrop. As I exited my apartment,ss I would cross paths immediately with the bustling cable cars, it was a fun steep walk down California street but it was cheery alright.

One day I got a call from a friend of the family, a Swedish lady fully credentialed type. She was a bonafide professional, an MBA in business, self-made executive living in a high-rise in Nob Hill. Catalina was her name. She rang me and said she had someone she would like me to meet.

She painted out the man in question to be an Iranian prince, he was a rich guy who owned a venture capitalist co-loved to play tennis and she claimed jaw dropping good looking. A few things I've picked up along the way in life is that people exaggerate. I figured I didn't have anything to lose but some time, I wanted to meet the Iranian prince. We met at the Ritz Carlton one day, had sandwiches and tea in the parlor. I think he had gotten the impression that I was from a refinedbackground. Little did he know I was the descendant from a Swedish slumlord.

At first glance, his looks didn't match Catalina's description (of course not). As I approached him, I could see he was far from Mr. Handsome pants. He sported a comb-over type haircut and had some skin peeling off his nose/chin. It looked like a rash, scaly. He was wearing a members-only t-shirt that was labeled as dating him way back into the 80's. I was barely born at that time, but I remember the fashion for some reason. We exchanged some small talk about what he did, what I was doing, my love for art, and his love for money. I had met some trust funder types before, but he was of the older variety. We ended up going on a series of dates until he invited me one day to his penthouse in Pacific Heights. His penthouse was on the top floor, and as he took me for a tour, it was clear he was some sort of a prince. You had to be very rich to own an apartment like that. His neighbor was Danielle Steele, after all. The highlight of our dating was an invitation to a July 4th party at his parents' penthouse. I arrived fashioned as best as I could with my budget- I couldn't really show up in a ball gown or something impressive to make a statement. A harpist was playing, and Hors D'oeuvres were being passed around by the waitstaff. I mixed and mingled and did what I could to mix in with the upper-crust set of people (mostly over 75). At one point, a lady I had been chatting with spilled an entire glass of red wine on the white carpet. It was like visiting a murder scene, seeing a white carpet drenched with red wine, looking like the victim's blood. People enjoyed the fireworks, overlooking the most impressive view I had seen in the Bay Area. The guest party stood on the balcony and took it all in. Nothing else developed with the venture capitalist after that night. It was clear I was definitely not his type, and he wasn't mine either.

Either way, I chalked it up as another San Francisco event. I got to see the most beautiful fireworks display and red wine on the white carpet tragedy- it wasn't a complete fluke.

On to the next. No Iranian connection here.

Bridesmaid-en

I was a bridesmaid to-be for a Latin-style wedding for a couple of college friends. I was to meet the others at a dinner party for the bachelorette Carmencita. I wandered around the area for several blocks, considering what to do while I waited for the rest of the group to surface. I ducked into a cafe to grab a drink and change into a more suitable dress. I made myself at home by plugging in my hot hair straightener, changing, doing my hair, and applying some makeup in the restroom. It was almost time to head to Pasha's, a Middle-

Eastern joint that the crew was scheduled to meet. I sat around and chatted with Amir, the waiter who was suitably fashioned with his shiny beaded Turkish vest and bright blue turban. He told me business was down, and he was used to at least 100 people in the rest. But now it was more like 20 or so. Times have changed, Amir stated and proceeded to inquire about my whereabouts and other chit-chat. I looked over at the bar and zoomed into the Turkish TV, which was playing TXT. It was a rendition of the full house but of a Turkish variety, with the intros consisting of a family skipping around their very minimally furnished living room that had a 70's looking decor to it.

A few moments later, Carmenita (the bride-to-be) peeked into the doorway holding an inflatable pink plastic penis while wearing a varied outfit that consisted of wings, tap-on condoms, misc. Additionally, all the rest of her friends and family members entered after her (the Spanish crew). The night began to roll as we drank, ate, and shared stories mostly involving dating men. It was a real-life rendition of the view with opinionated suburban pregnant women and some others tossed in. The entertainment consisted of some belly dancers and a very American tradition of the conga line routine. I did my best to power through the experience. I did have thoughts of bolting the scene with some excuse, but it was too complicated.

We continued to the Embassy Suites, a worn-trodden hotel located in the suburbs of San Francisco. It had a Denny-style buffet breakfast available and a dingy swimming pool with remnants of trash littered along the side from the previous night's binging episode. The bride's to-be family from Spain had arrived, and you could hear their presence as their loud Spanish voices echoed through the halls. She had a tight-knit group from her homeland, as it appeared in those countries. People were like family, pretty tight. I didn't experience that through my stages of bouncing around different school yards. In America, my experience was people are cliquish and segmented off. If you were a cheerleader, you only hung with that specific crowd, so you had better get your high kicks down and on point to belong in on their scene. I skipped around with theater people/art's crowd. In retrospect, I wish I had been more athletic. I liked smoking cigarettes and would spend my lunch breaks in the stalls of bathrooms. I ended up getting busted by Ms. Pellerman, the lesbian volleyball coach. I wasn't able to get rid of the smoke. However, quickly, I tossed my cig into the toilet. Back then, I didn't cut the athletics department. I failed gym for not wearing the right colored shorts. They were navy, but with plaid underneath, it didn't pass.

The night really began to take flight as the entire crew set out to WLPJ's local nightclub located at the outskirts of suburban hell. It featured 80s music and an assortment of locals from the area in attendance. A motley crew crowd, mullet cuts, rumpled 80's band t-shirt-wearing crowd. As I stood by the bar and waited to order my one drink that was complimentary being a part of the wedding party, the bar lady who resembled Rosie Odonnell with biker chick fashion sense turned to me and shouted, "You need to learn some patience, honey," After standing in the same spot for over twenty minutes watching her pour about ten drinks, five shots, and a dozen blended margaritas, I think anyone's patience would have been tried.

Nevertheless, I made my way over to the dance floor and embraced one of the guests named Abby, who was looking to dance. I wanted to cut all my losses for the evening with a dance. He danced so quickly with rapid movements, twisting and turning like nobody's business. He wore a silk blue shirt, neatly pressed blue trousers, and cuff links. He reminded me of a young Fred Astaire with sparkling blue eyes and the rhythm that was gonna get you. I whispered in his ear that he would do well in downtown San Francisco and his target audience would shower him with adoration. I had seen it first hand after my time with the gap model in the Castro. I could be his agent and earn some commission on the proceeds, I thought to myself. Maybe this could be my next calling? Scouting out effeminate men to bring to the Castro and see how we could do. I wouldn't be a madam of sorts but just a liaison for connection.

Made in the USA
Middletown, DE
10 January 2025

69180798R00020